a minus tide

novella by robin beeman

CHRONICLE BOOKS
SAN FRANCISCO

Printed in the United States of America.

ISBN: 0-8118-1090-9

Library of Congress Cataloging-in-Publication Data available.

Book and jacket design: Pamela Geismar
Composition: Neal Elkin, On Line Typography
Cover photograph © 1995 Daniel Proctor

Distributed in Canada by Raincoast Books,
8680 Cambie Street, Vancouver, B.C. V6P 6M9

10 9 8 7 6 5 4 3 2 1

Chronicle Books
275 Fifth Street
San Francisco, CA 94103

for elmer

evan

There were these three trees, Douglas firs, on the west side of the house, tall things, not ancient but big enough to be taken seriously, and in the winter when the storms came in over the ridge from the Pacific, they swayed pretty crazily—always toward the house. If we'd had a lot of rain you could see them lifting their roots, soil and all, as they swayed. Mattie hated that swaying. She said the firs presented a danger to us or at least the house, a big old shingled place built as a farmhouse in the twenties, with a view west across a meadow to a grove of trees on the opposite hill. In storms, firs did come down on a regular basis, it's true. In the big storm three years ago one crashed through the roof of the house of an old woman down the road, pinning her in bed. She could have been killed. A few inches this way or that. A neighbor at the bend of the road had one come through the kitchen roof as she was making soup while seven or eight piled up like pickup sticks beside the house. Redwoods tend not to fall. Sometimes their tops snap off in a high wind but they tend to stay planted.

You can limb trees, of course. All that greenery at the top acts like a sail. If you cut out enough limbs the wind passes right on through without taking the tree along. It makes sense. The tree man explained it to us and Mattie said, "Fine, limb the redwoods but take out the firs." She was adamant. And yet the thought of taking out the trees made us sad. When you live up here in the hills for a while you begin to understand that the trees belong here more than we do. You can let them be or you can get this competitive thing with them. "It's them versus us," I said, trying to be funny. "They can fall on us but we've got the chainsaws."

"That's ugly," said Mattie, "but true."

~

Sally arrived on the day after they'd come down, a February day, chilly and overcast. The tree man had offered us a better price if we did the clean up so Sally came upon us standing in what looked like a battlefield, Mattie and me the victors with the hacked-up corpses of the firs, limbs and trunks all around. I was splitting rounds and Mattie was stacking. We'd have several cords when it was done.

We heard a shriek and looked up. Sally stood on the deck, a California version of the Munch painting, mouth open and contorted, her hands to her head. We hadn't seen Sally in ten or so years—she had this way of disappearing then turning up as if no time had passed in between—so neither of us was surprised that it was Sally making the noise. Sally could be dramatic, a beautiful woman given to acting out. She and Mattie looked a lot alike but Sally was a slimmer more delicate version. Mattie has big bones and a solidity that I like. She's not heavy but she takes up space in a sculptural way. Gratifyingly three dimensional, like one of those hefty bronzes you want to run your hands over. Next to Mattie, Sally is a paper doll.

"I know it's a mess," said Mattie.

"It's murder," said Sally. "Their souls are swirling around right over your head. I can see them even if you can't. It's hideous."

Mattie sighed and placed the log rather more carefully than she would have without Sally standing there, probably to taunt Sally, before she walked up the steps. Sally allowed herself to be hugged.

"She's probably right about the trees," I said to Mattie in bed that night. "I do feel all this swirling angst."

"I think that's Sally you feel." Sally had taken up residence in Cammie's room right across the hall.

"They might well have souls," I said.

"I expect they do. And I feel dreadful. But I did believe

they threatened us—in a perfectly innocent way, of course—without malevolence on their part."

~

At breakfast the next morning I found Mattie at the kitchen window staring out. "So much light," she said. "I never expected so much light out there."

I walked over and stood beside her. She was right about the light. What before had been a dense weave of jutting branches, green needles, gray bark—an almost viscous shade—had given way to a hard insistent light. We both shivered.

Two months later Sally would be dead and Mattie and I would be struggling to make sense of what had happened to us.

mattie

hundreds of feet down the white Toyota rested on the sand, caught between two large boulders, its wheels in the air, casual as a dropped toy. Beyond the car stretched the ocean, cobalt streaked with aquamarine dutifully receding toward a lambent horizon, the plane of water, the plane of sky two big luminous blocks of space pushing outward. I thought I remembered hearing that the distance to the horizon is three miles for a person standing on the shore. There's a formula for this, of course. How far was it to the horizon from this height? How high did you have to get to be able to see what was coming before it appeared on the horizon itself? Along the base of the cliff ran a ribbon of gunpowder gray sand and beyond that sparkled a rug of uncovered seaweed mottled by glistening tide pools.

The sheriff had called me because the car was still registered in my name. Sally had needed a car when she arrived so I'd given her my old reliable Toyota. It seems she hadn't bothered to change the registration. By the time I got to the cliff the ambulance had already taken her body back to town.

"There's a minus tide now so the water's extra low," said the deputy, a thin blondish man with dark glasses over his eyes and pink puffy lips. I knew about such things but I didn't interrupt. "The accident must have happened early this morning when the tide was up for there to have been enough water in the cab for her to drown, if she did drown, that is, if she wasn't killed going down. A couple of abalone divers found her. There was a fifth of vodka without a top and a carton of orange juice, both filled with seawater."

The abalone divers were giving the Toyota a respectful ring of space, their black-suited bodies figures of mourning, their submersions into the water a ritual of purification. "She liked to drive and drink," I said. "You'll probably find a commuter cup too. She'd put that on the seat beside her and pour in half vodka and half-orange juice."

"A commuter cup didn't turn up. The window was open and it probably fell out when the car rolled over. She wasn't wearing a seatbelt." He appeared distressed rather than disapproving when he said this. "We get a lot of these things here on the coast. More than you'd think. There's almost always alcohol involved."

"I don't think safety was that important to her."

The deputy shook his head. "About a year ago a man crawled up out of a wreck a few miles north of here. He said he'd had time to reconsider things as he rolled over. He'd wanted to do himself in but then halfway down he changed his mind. It was too late for anything other than prayer, he said. So he prayed and the next thing you know he's out of the car on a little ledge and the car is still going down."

"I guess my sister didn't change her mind," I said.

When I pulled away from the edge of the cliff I headed back south for a mile or so and then turned inland onto a steep road that wound up to the top of the ridge where it ran parallel to the coast, dipping into groves of trees and then coming out into sudden bright clearings where sheep grazed. I turned left into a driveway leading to a small log cabin in deep redwood shade. I'd been here with Sally about six weeks ago. I'd had a day off from teaching so she asked if I wanted to take a drive. I'd mentioned to her my surprise that the cabin, despite its location on the top of the ridge, had no view of the ocean when a simple amount of clearing, lopping of low-hanging branches, would have opened a window. "Joel's not that kind of person," Sally had said. "He likes to have to walk a little to find the view. He doesn't want to take the ocean for granted."

Joel hadn't been there that day so I didn't meet him. Sally

must have known he wouldn't be but I think she wanted me to
see the place, to approve of it somehow and by extension to
approve of Joel. In truth I hadn't liked the cabin or its situation.
Though the cabin was well built there was something willfully
dank and unappealing about it. "It's probably very pleasant inside," I said and she knew everything.

She didn't reply to this but offered, "I do appreciate the car,
you know, Mattie. I don't know what I'd do without you."

This time Joel was there. Sally had told me that he often
worked in the cabin because he found his office too distracting.
I'd been calm with the deputy on the cliff but now as I knocked
on the door I trembled. "I'm Sally's sister," I said as the door
opened and Joel, taller and bulkier than I'd expected, bent his
head to me like an adult to a child. Even in the dimness I could
tell that his color was bad—one of those people who go
mauve when they don't sleep. I felt that he already knew about
Sally though that seemed unlikely. I was the only person the
sheriff's office called.

"I'm sure you are," he said attempting a smile. "You look a
great deal like her." I could see how easy it would be under
different circumstances to find him charming. "This is about
Sally?"

I managed to nod yes and my expression gave the rest away.

"Oh, God," he moaned.

"Over the cliff, right below here." My teeth began to chat-
ter. I saw a woodstove in the corner and I felt the heat in the

room. More than anything I wanted to go over and hold my hands to the stove but Joel stepped between me and the entry.

"I'm very sorry but I have to be alone right now," he said backing into the room. With a bow, a brusque attempt at both formality and dismissal, he closed the door in my face.

In the car I pushed the heater to full blast. I'd go north then take another side road down to the coast highway again. This is what Sally must have done so I'd do it too, going over the path of the last miles of hers in order to understand what had happened. The deputy had spoken of it as an accident first, then treated it as somehow intentional, a suicide, guiding me to think of it as he did though I hadn't wanted to. I would have preferred to think Sally had been reckless, not desperate.

Though I didn't know for certain, I think that Sally must have been at Joel's earlier that night. I imagined her leaving Joel's and going north as I was, looping around onto the coast highway so that she would be heading south in the lane beside the ocean. I drove along the edge for about two and a half miles wondering how often she'd driven this stretch in the daylight and when the idea of going over occurred.

Not that the idea of going over doesn't occur involuntarily to almost everyone who drives this. The road is a narrow two lanes with even narrower shoulders, and the drop over the western edge is a long one. With enough alcohol for misjudgment almost any outer turn could be misgauged, explaining many accidents as simply that—terrible miscalculations. But

mattie
9

the deputy had believed it a suicide as if he had a nose for such things, a way to sniff out the truth.

I passed a barricade on one such turn where the road had almost washed away in a recent rain. At another turn the curve seemed right though when I stopped to look down I saw that the land did not fall away but descended gently in hills covered with clumps of lavender lupine and chrome yellow mustard. I crossed a cattle guard and came upon Sally's spot behind the police cones. The curve was banked but with a certain amount of speed a car could leap the low berm. I parked and got out of the car again to look. If you took the curve a little late there was an outcrop of land to stop the fall. If you took it too early there was a shelf of earth below, a landslide from earlier. To actually plunge directly as Sally had all the way to the water took either very bad luck or planning. When I'd come to that conclusion, I began to sob. Only my tears weren't for Sally.

joel

there's a Gerard Manley Hopkins poem Anna read me. Anna's fond of Hopkins and I find I like him myself. He's ardent and mystical, much like Anna. Hopkins' poem is "Spring and Fall" and it's addressed to a young child grieving over the petals falling from a flower. The poet addresses Margaret, the child, telling her that though she'll come to much worse sights in the future, the source of sorrow for all things we mourn is the same. In the final couplet he says, *It is the blight man was born for / It is Margaret you mourn for.*

Anna calls the blight original sin. I call it simply not being immortal. We all mourn our own fates when we mourn any death. Our grief is for ourselves, for the fact that we must die.

It's a fine poem, unleaving like the flower, down to the essential cold core of certainty. Hopkins was a priest and I imagine he believed in a hereafter. Anna was a nun almost a century later and I'm not sure what she believes is on the other side. I don't believe there is another side. My parents were radicals, members of the left, supporters of Communism until they found out about Stalin, and atheists. I've never been comfortable with atheism. I do believe that good deeds in this world are important, however, if only because they improve the lot of humanity. I'm a bleeding heart liberal coming down on the side of the underdog.

I'm always on the prowl, says Anna, for women who'll need my services. Anna is my third wife. We'd separated right before Sally appeared. I'd begun seeing another woman, before the separation, actually, and that hadn't sat well with Anna—not that I blame her.

Over the years I've discovered that women like me. Ursine is the word I choose to use to describe myself, only now the bear is gray rather than black. I've always felt feral. I like to sniff the air, smell the earth, identify people by their scents. I'm not unhappy being part of the animal kingdom. I think this acknowledgement of mine that I'm an animal helps me attract women. Women of a certain kind, the kind that, happily, I'm also attracted to. Fey women. Women not terribly attached to the earth. We recognize our opposites in the other. Anna would be different, but I wouldn't learn this until later.

On the day I first met Anna, when she told me she'd once been a nun, it knocked me out. Here was this beautiful woman in jeans and a plaid shirt standing beside a family of farm workers—mother, father, and six children in the van. Anna had called out of the blue to ask if she could come by my office and talk to me.

"Mr. Stone, I'd like you to meet Mr. and Mrs. Torres," she said an hour later, standing on a patch of lawn in front of my office. She then proceeded to introduce each child by name: Felipe, Luz, Teresa, Octavio, Milagro, Conchita, and Geronimo, the baby in Mrs. Torres' arms. We exchanged formalities, and formalities is the right word. The Torres family was solemn and courteous and I tried to rise to their standards. I can be an oaf at times.

Mrs. Torres had a problem relating to her last delivery, which took place in the back seat of their car on the way from Gilroy to Soledad, between lettuce and asparagus. Mr. Torres had a hernia. Milagro had crossed eyes. Octavio had some sort of difficulty breathing. All of them needed inoculations. They were proud, however, and added firmly that they wanted to pay for whatever help they received. Only, of course, there was no way they could. They'd arrived here for the apples and would move north later to the pears. It was a hot August day. The traffic droned by behind us.

With the Torres family in the back, Anna, whom I was able to study in profile because she was driving, took me to a small town a few miles north where the beginning of a clinic had set up shop in an old five-and-dime store. Nickled and dimed, I thought as I entered. That's what these people get almost anywhere they go. They pay exorbitant prices to live in shacks, if they can find a shack, and from there debt piles on debt. The winery growers are the worst since they make the most from their laborers' efforts. They have no shame about letting their workers sleep under bridges or in the woods on a roadside. At a recent local wine auction a case of wine sold for sixty-thousand dollars. Quite a difference from the four dollars and twenty-five cents an hour pickers make— if they're lucky.

The inside of the store had been partitioned and painted white with blue trim. The walls of the waiting room were decorated with posters of Zapata, Cesar Chavez, Dolores Huerta, and the Virgin of Guadalupe blessing a group of kneeling farm workers, as well as by nice reproductions of some of Diego Rivera's social protest murals. A young Latino woman who spoke English sat at the front desk. Three people waited, all men, all dusty from the fields, all with their straw hats on their knees. Behind one panel was an examining room with a nurse practitioner, a volunteer. Anna and I talked to the nurse, and the Torres family took the rest of the seats in the waiting room. This would be the first medical examination any of the children had ever received.

"You must see how necessary this place is," said Anna, turning her eyes on me, eyes with a glow behind them like the flame of a lamp behind blue glass.

"I'll do everything in my power to help," I said.

"That's good news," said the nurse, a thirtyish woman with a broad sun-tanned face and a reassuring stance. "Anna got us a start-up grant but it doesn't cover much and it won't last forever."

"We'll get what we need," said Anna to me, shrugging this off. "I was a nun for years and I like to think I know how to pray."

Terrific, I thought, both spiritual and practical. She'd begun straightening up the room for the next patient, her movements economical yet graceful, while the nurse made notes in a file.

Driving me back to my office, Anna was quiet. I knew next to nothing about nuns but I imagined her praying all alone in a dim cathedral, her hands clasped, the scent of incense and the glow of candles in the background, her face raised to a stained-glass widow, the rose window in Chartres, her perfect cheek-bones and clear high forehead framed by the starched white coif. I imagined her eyes glazing over in ecstasy as she stretched out her arms, the power of her ecstasy lifting her above the stone floor and holding her suspended. My heart pounded against its rib cage and I felt myself grow lighter. Astonishing. Also very erotic.

I kept my word. Anna addressed the groups I belonged to and like a magician drew large checks, including mine, from usually closed checkbooks. Her clear-eyed conviction was irresistible. After each meeting I took her to dinner in some posh place to celebrate. She ate like a horse, which delighted me, and drank too—nothing excessive, but with gusto. She has a wild raucous laugh.

We made love after the third of these dinners. I took her to my cabin up on the coast. It was a cold September evening and I made a fire in the wood stove and poured brandy for us and put Joe Cocker on the CD. She knew the songs. We sang together. I kissed her, and the light from the rose window struck us both. "I might become a believer," I said when she snuggled herself against me in bed afterward. I'd had some idea that I might be her first but I wasn't. I never found out who the first was. Anna's a private person.

anna

the class was community organizing with a strong dose of liberation theology. Mark stood in front of a portable chalk board in the back room of a migrant workers services center. Dust that never seemed to settle hovered in the valley heat outside the windows. The students were the usual assortment of people who get involved in work like this. I was there with Veronica, another woman from my convent, both of us on a year's leave of absence. We'd been teaching in a parochial school in the South Bay that was closed by the bishop because it couldn't support itself, so we were looking for other opportunities to be of service. We'd been recruited by Father Mark, although no one in the class called him Father. He'd received a research grant from several organizations interested in doing good, and we were paid a small allotment and given housing with local people who supported our work. Besides Veronica and me, there were two older white-haired Quaker women who'd done this sort of thing in Latin America, three college students—two young men and a woman, all radicals with fervent eyes and lots of theory—and a very taciturn young man who always wore a starched white shirt. Veronica and I suspected him of being a spy.

"Our work is to go out into the community and talk to people, not just the farm workers but anyone who might be involved with them in any way—teachers, employers, doctors and nurses, legal aid workers, ministers, social workers, grocers. Use your imagination," Mark said, leaning on his hands over his desk. "We need to determine what the population is and what their needs are. We want the workers and the people who deal with the workers to tell us what services could help them best. We don't want to approach this survey with preconceived ideas." We all nodded but each of us knew this last was just talk. We had models already of what we could and probably would do. "Local input is important," he said. We nodded again. We had a day-care center and a health clinic in mind.

Mark wore a plaid shirt and jeans and sneakers like someone wearing the clothes of an adopted country. No matter how casual he tried to look, I always saw him in a Roman collar.

Maybe it was the way he held his head, a little higher than a man in an open neck shirt needed to. When he walked, I saw the invisible black soutane swinging beside his ankles. He was small-boned, with copper hair and that very pink skin that goes with the hair. When he went out into the fields to talk to the workers he wore a baseball cap and sweated profusely. He'd grown up in the foggy western side of San Francisco and regarded the sun as a device put in the sky to test him and his commitment. Time and time again I thought he'd fall over from heat stroke. He kept a cooler of Seven-Up in the back of the van which he guzzled as he drove. The van, of course, had no air-conditioning.

Mark and I became lovers after our second week of working together. Mark had just broken up with a married woman. The guilt must have been driving them both nuts. I wasn't married and that I know was a great relief to him. The fact that I was a nun made it seem almost sanctioned. He was a passionate man in his work and in his love-making, and I fell in love with him like a school girl, ridiculously, embarrassingly, hungrily. He rented a small house on the edge of town. The living room served as his office. At night I went there to go over the day's surveys with him. One night after we had put the surveys aside and sat outside in the coolness drinking beers, he put his arm around my shoulders—a companionable gesture. We knew we liked each other. Then he kissed my cheek. Then he turned my face and kissed my lips. I put my hand behind his head and kissed him back. We were in bed in a matter of minutes. My first time. "This is sacred too," he said afterward, kissing my hair.

At the end of the summer I knew I would leave the convent. I wanted Mark to marry me. I believe he loved me but his vocation won out and he gave me up. An affair was one thing. A wife was another. "I'm a priest," he said. "I've taken vows." I hadn't been wrong about the Roman collar and soutane.

On our last night a group of people we'd worked most closely with invited us to a fiesta in the pool room in the back of a bar called Mi Ranchito. The single men brought girls, all dressed in bright dresses with high hair-dos and lots of make-up, and the married couples came with their children, washed and polished, the little girls with hair ribbons, the little boys with water-parted hair. There was crepe paper and homemade tamales and chicken mole and tortillas. Near midnight, when I thought it was over, a mariachi band arrived and we danced. Boys and girls, Veronica and me, the young woman student and the Quakers with all of the men, Mark and the young men students with the women. The spy did not show up.

"You've been having an affair with Father Mark," Veronica said when the two of us had stepped outside to cool off. It wasn't a question. He'd danced with every one but me by then. Veronica was older than I was, a practical, straight-forward woman. I don't know why it hadn't occurred to me that she might suspect. Veronica and I didn't live together, but earlier in the summer we had spent our free evenings together. Then I'd started working on each day's surveys with Mark.

"Yes, but it's over."

"Good," she said. "I'm not drawn to men myself, but I can see that he's not right for you."

"He's a priest," I said.

"And a very good one at that." She gave me an odd smile, a little pitying, I thought, but very kind.

A couple of years later, when I met Joel, the project I was working on then was very much the same. Our goal was to establish a clinic where Spanish would be spoken and where fees would be collected based on a sliding scale, sliding down to nothing in most cases. I'm still working with the clinic though now I'm on the board of a foundation that receives grant money from private charities and allocates the money to local projects. We now have a day-care center, a nutrition project, and a legal aid center—to which Joel still gives a great deal of time.

It's work I love and I think, despite the fact that I have a husband and two children, that I am the same person I was at the beginning of the summer I met Mark, before I planned to leave the convent for good. It's an odd thing to say. I don't think many people would admit to having been unchanged by their experiences, although that's not what I mean, either. It's just that Mark knew he shouldn't marry. I didn't have the wisdom

to know that about myself then. I wasn't supposed to marry
and have children. I love my children, you understand, but they
don't seem like mine, really. They seem much more Joel's. I
feel like a mother on loan to them, like I'm a bit of a fraud.

a
minus
tide

e v a n

"It began with the trees," I said after the service.

"Chronology doesn't impose causality," said Mattie. I loved her for that, for her reasonableness. We sat on the deck in the still unfamiliar afternoon sunlight. The huge rhododendrons which had been here when we'd bought the place were all in bloom, a sight that has always nudged us to fits of admiration and praise. "It just happened."

"Thank you," I said.

I knew that the trees had nothing to do with Sally's death but the memory of Sally screaming on the deck, which had struck me as ludicrous when it happened, now seemed to have been ominous. When Sally left ten years ago I knew I was part

of the reason for her departure, though the situation that pro-
voked it even now seems slight. So slight I never thought of it
until she mentioned it on her return. I'd been relieved when
she left and I'd put the bad business behind me.

Ten years ago Sally accused me of stealing her bicycle, and I

still can't understand how she got things so wrong. The way I
remembered it she'd given me the bicycle, a fairly decent but
much used ten-speed she seldom rode, to exchange for some
dope. When I came back with the dope, she wanted to know
what I'd done with her bike, and I said something like, "Come
on Sally, you told me to take it and try to trade it for some
dope for you and dope for me. That was the deal. Your bike,
my connection. Remember? You gave me the bike."

"You stole the bicycle," she screamed. The same scream as
on the deck, mouth in a twisted O, hands to her head.

"You're hysterical, Sally, calm down." She was living in a
disgusting little trailer then and working as a waitress —
a woman with a good mind and a college education yelling
about a lousy bike and a couple of lids of dope like some crazed
street person. Not only was she screaming, she was also
pounding on my chest and I was trying to fend her off. When
she kicked my shin I gave her a shove and she wound up falling
backward onto the couch.

Nothing hard but it startled her and she stopped screaming,
looking more surprised than anything, surprised not just to
have stopped screaming but to be where she was, which as I

said was a pretty nasty place. Small and cramped, with forests of mildew which she tried to mask by burning incense sticks. She had the windows covered with an orange India print cloth.

"I feel like Peter, Peter, pumpkin eater in this dump," I said. She started to laugh. Hysterical again but easier to take. Then she calmed down and we smoked some of the stuff which was so powerful it pushed the back of my head out about a mile. I started to laugh too, and then we wound up fucking. I'd always thought Sally was great looking but I'd never been attracted to her. Mattie had me all tied up in that department. It had never occurred to me before that afternoon to lust after Sally. We did the deed and it was okay—not great—but it felt friendly. Then we ate some stale chocolate cake she had in a cupboard and I went home. I thought she'd understood the bike deal and that was that.

So it was strange when after she gets back from her ten year trip around the world—India, Thailand, Bali, places like that—and she's living with me and Mattie until she can find a place of her own, that she brings up the stolen bike to me as the reason she left. I could have thought of better reasons like you made love to your sister's husband and you were ashamed to look your sister in the face. Oddly, I hadn't felt guilty then for sleeping with Sally. It felt friendly, not sordid. I didn't tell Mattie though.

By the time Sally got back I hadn't smoked dope in years. It just stopped being fun, so I quit. I guess Sally quit too, but somewhere she started really drinking. It had been beer and wine before but when she came out of Cammie's bedroom on the evening of the scene about the trees I smelled real alcohol on her breath. I know they say you can't smell vodka but there was this cool sweetness in the air. She held the neck of a guitar in her hand.

Mattie had fixed a typical Mattie meal — too much of everything and all good. I think this meal was Dungeness crab, in honor of Sally's return, and a big salad and some sort of pasta and vegetables and a nice mellow Chardonnay. Candles, their mother's damask tablecloth, camellias floating in a bowl — the whole ball of wax. A little celebration for the re-turn of the prodigal.

Sally didn't eat the crab — she'd become a vegetarian in the interim — but she polished off the Chardonnay and most of another bottle. Afterward we sat around and Sally began strumming the guitar. Chords. She looked dreamy, which I attributed to the booze. Then she started singing some song about crystal skies and butterflies and this and that. Minor key. I didn't recall ever having heard her sing before. A nice enough voice if part of a sing-along but not a voice that can re-ally stand on its own. It was a light soprano — very light — which she attempted to disguise by whispering a lot in a way that was supposed to be intriguing. She'd made up the lyrics and the tune, and truly it was more than a little depressing — not because it was actually so bad but because I could tell this was so important to her.

"Good stuff," I said, and Mattie said, "That's terrific, sweetie." Sally announced that she's been singing in clubs in Fiji or Tahiti or somewhere and she was going to look for a job singing in a club around here. I got this pit-of-the-stomach feeling and Mattie said something non-committal about most of the musicians she knew around here having day jobs.

Then Sally asked about clubs and I mentioned some and so did Mattie, and then Sally said she wanted us all to go. Mattie begged off. She always gets up early in the morning to paint and she had a show coming up in a couple of weeks, a show in a gallery she'd been courting for years. It was a big thing and nobody worked harder than Mattie because she didn't just paint for herself, she had to go to the college and teach the lit- tle wannabes how to paint too.

So it was Mattie who insisted I take Sally.

We drove downtown to Hurry Up, a bar with a small stage where the fair to middling local acts play on weeknights. I think it was jazz on Tuesdays, folk on Wednesdays, Thursdays were for comics. At the bar we run into Joel Stone. Joel and I had shot some baskets together years ago when we'd both just moved up from San Francisco and I guess we liked each other. He'd become a hot-shot criminal lawyer while I'd never really gotten the employment habit down. I was always doing one thing or another, usually selling. It's been office supplies for a while. So our paths rarely crossed much any more. But this is a friendly community, proud of the fact that it isn't income conscious.

Joel and I were cordial and I introduced him to Sally. Joel had been married but I'd heard he and his wife were separated so I wasn't particularly surprised when he and Sally took an interest in each other. Joel's tall with a barrel chest, a little heavy, with lots of curly hair and those liquid dark eyes women seem to like, and Sally was a nice looking woman. She had on tight jeans and a T-shirt and some sort of ethnic jacket, kind of bulky with silver threads through it. There was some gray in her long brown hair which looked good—a little like Emmylou Harris, sexy—and which complemented the silver threads in her jacket. So I left them at the bar to go play darts. It was jazz night, a young woman on the piano. Cool, understated. An hour or so later Sally came looking for me, all beamy and more than a little tipsy. Good, I thought. Mattie'll be glad that Sally had some fun on her first night back. Mattie is very protective of Sally even though Sally annoys the hell out of her eighty percent of the time.

Joel had been great to her, she said. He'd introduced her to the owner and she was going to audition for folk night the very next afternoon. "I told him I was a little like Joni Mitchell," she said, still beamy. Whatever, I thought, though I said something positive like, "You'll wow him."

It was on the way back, out of the blue, she mentioned the bicycle again. I blamed it on the liquor, but I was amazed that she could still summon up such rancor after all those years. "You never were trustworthy," she said. "I can't believe Mattie stayed with you—a lying loser, two-timing vain shallow asshole."

"Wait a minute," I said. I hadn't had all that much to drink. In truth, my substance abuse days are behind me, something I can feel good about, but I was walloped by what she said, by the tone mostly, the viciousness. "I just took you out and introduced you to a guy who introduced you to a guy who's maybe going to give you a job. Is this your idea of a thank you?"

"You stole my bicycle. You came over and took it while I was at work and then you tried to pretend that I'd told you to take it for some lousy dope."

"Why would I have wanted your bicycle? It wasn't even a new one. I had to talk him into taking it. And the dope was excellent, by the way."

"You're fatuous too."

"Give us both a break, Sally. You've had too much to drink."

"Mattie was cheating on you at the same time. Really cheating—like big time. I'll bet you didn't know that."

"As a matter of fact I did. Mattie told me. It was a long time ago and we've put it aside." This isn't exactly the way I'd felt about it but close enough. It was history at any rate.

"You're not even honest with yourself."

"Listen, Sally. I heard you telling Mattie tonight that you'd been studying all these Eastern religions in your travels. Why don't you just lighten up, let go all this stuff you believe happened in the past. Isn't that what you're supposed to do with those religions?"

"Don't even presume," she said. Then she passed out. I was so glad she'd stopped talking I didn't mind carrying her into the house and putting her to bed. When I slid in beside Mattie, next to all that fleshy heat she puts off at night, and fit myself into the familiar contours, my nose in her shampoo-scented hair, I wondered why I hadn't mentioned to Sally the way she'd let herself off the hook for what she did with me, her own sister's husband.

When I left the next morning Sally was still asleep. When I came back she and Mattie were purring in the kitchen over some curried vegetable affair that would offer no roadblock to Sally's spiritual progress. It actually turned out to be tasty as well. We drank beer with it, Sally doing her share—beer, of course, being vegetable. Last night's nastiness seemed forgotten.

At eight, Sally went into Cammie's room and came out wearing a long eggplant-colored nightgowny dress and carrying a guitar case. She'd landed a spot for folk night, but she didn't want us to come yet she said because she needed a little time to feel sure of herself. Mattie and I agreed that this was a good idea and Sally drove herself off in Mattie's Toyota. A few days later Sally found a cottage to rent and moved out. According to Mattie there were several more gigs in the future.

"Amazing," I said.

"Well, maybe she was just nervous with us that night," said Mattie.

~

Mattie's show was a wild success. The gallery, a chi-chi place with a clientele from the city, was packed. Champagne, oozing cheeses, little fresh fruit tarts, lots of tanned skin, bleached teeth, and good posture. Mattie's watercolors are a delight, even when they're puzzling. Mostly they're landscapes but she's done away with perspective so that they're both pattern as well as scene. You can identify objects but their relationships to other objects startle you. Lots of bright colors. "Sophisticated primitives," said one reviewer. "Provocative and sensuous," said another. She sold a dozen right off the bat and the little red sold spots kept turning up.

Cammie dashed in to admire, though she'd seen most of the paintings already. "You're a wonder, Mom," she said. "A visionary." Mattie glowed. I put my arms around them both. Cammie looks like me rather than Mattie, long legged and skinny, with the same color hair, pineapple sherbert hair, Cammie calls it, and the same freckles. She adores Mattie and treats me in a casual off-hand way like a dear friend she finds amusing but inconsequential.

"Aren't you bursting, Dad?" she said, giving me an extra squeeze and tossing her hair in that insouciant way some girls seem to pick up in college. "Isn't Mom fantastic?" Then she rushed off to study for an exam the next morning. Right after she left Sally and Joel strolled in looking cozy and lustful at the same time. Joel bought a painting of a river climbing up a mountain—one I liked especially.

Mattie was giddy with success on the way home. She'd take the summer off, maybe take a leave the next year. Strangely, after having encouraged and emotionally sustained Mattie for what seemed like centuries, I felt let down and melancholy. When she went into the bathroom for a long post-celebration soak, I walked outside and sat on one of the stumps beside a pile of branches and boughs that we'd intended to burn but hadn't had time to. My own life was a dismal funk. Sally's insults looped over and over again on a short nasty little tape in my brain. I started to cry. Foul, maudlin, self-pitying tears.

mattie

Several years ago I left Evan and went to Italy with my lover who was dying from a brain tumor. It was a terribly romantic act. Keats had died in Italy of tuberculosis. Shelley had drowned off the Italian coast. Romantic and ghastly.

Gordon left his wife and three small children and I left Evan and eleven-year-old Cammie. At the time I told myself that what Gordon left was more significant, more wrenching, but in Italy I began to believe otherwise. Gordon no longer loved his wife and scarcely acknowledged his children except to provide for them in an distant, indifferent way. I loved Evan and Cammie. I'd told Cammie that I'd gotten a fellowship to study art in Florence which she believed, and which Evan never contradicted. I'd accepted that if I came home and Evan wouldn't take me back, not only would I lose him but Cammie would have to learn the truth.

In Italy, Gordon proceeded to worsen almost immediately. The doctors in California had given a month. He scarcely had three weeks. The first week we spent in Florence, which was hot, dusty, smoggy, and noisy. We'd taken rooms in a pension across the Arno but noise carries over water—Vespas, horns, voices, loudspeakers. The river was low and debris floated on the surface.

Pale gold dust, the same color as the ancient buildings, veiled the trees. We took taxis to the square beside the Palazzo Vecchio and drank cappuccinos and took very short walks to the Uffizi. In the Academy we admired the Michelangelos but it was hard for me to watch Gordon looking up at all the unfinished pieces, searching for unclaimed form still locked up in marble.

The second week I rented a car and drove us to Siena, which was cooler and quieter. When his vision wasn't blurring, Gordon managed some sketches, lovely delicate things. Most people would never guess from his huge abstract paintings what a gift for line he had. I did nothing but hover. "Don't think you have to be heroic," he said one afternoon on a little terrace outside of our room. "Walk, walk, steal some flowers from a nobleman's garden. You needn't keep watch."

"I'm not being heroic, you are," I murmured.

"No," he said. "I'm doing exactly what I want to do."

That evening we made our way down the cobbled street to a little restaurant which our pension recommended. Gordon had soup and bread and I had everything. It was the first time since I'd gotten to Italy that I'd had an appetite. I ate pasta and fish and chicken, each dish more delicious than the last. I drank a bottle of wine by myself. He watched me with an amused smile, encouraging me to eat more and more, to gorge, to order a fresh bottle of wine. I did, eating and drinking for him, for myself, for the whole famished world. "That was wonderful," he said when they brought the bill and I sat in my chair, holding onto the seat to keep from reeling over sideways. I tottered up the cobbled street to the hotel leaning on him, onto the little that remained of his flesh. I remember him chuckling as we lay side by side in bed.

In the morning I found that he'd fallen into a coma during his sleep. We went by ambulance to a hospital in Rome where they spoke English. In Rome I did finally walk, and walk — into huge dim churches to light candles, so many candles, trusting their sturdy little flames the way I couldn't trust my words to plea for a gentle death for Gordon. Then I walked down long cool corridors to his room and saw that the candles were doing their work. Though he lay immobilized under a net of tubes, Gordon looked serene. He never recovered consciousness.

I was devastated by the simple fluidity of his going, by how little I'd been able to do for him. I'd girded myself to become someone heroic—he'd been right about that—and I felt paltry instead, paltry and dazed.

Coming back home might have been disastrous if I'd been less dazed. As it was, some vestigial guidance system in my brain took over and got me and Gordon's coffin on a plane. Gordon's wife met me at the airport in San Francisco to receive the coffin, a pretty plump woman with stout blond braids and a closed face. She was civil to me, grateful actually, as if I'd done her a favor by taking him away and bringing him back contained as he was. "He's going back to Illinois to the town where he grew up," she said. "His brother's arriving tomorrow."

"His death was very peaceful," I said. "He just slipped away."

"That's good," she said, as if approving of the job I'd done. "Gordon didn't like pain." For the first time I saw how their marriage must have been for her and how relieved she was that it was over.

At home Evan asked no questions. I fell back into the role I'd played before and we never spoke about what I'd done, as if I hadn't done it. We were both wary, however, and the wariness continued—except when we made love. There it dissolved.

I didn't cry for Gordon in Rome because I was too stunned by disbelief, and back home I couldn't cry because to mourn Gordon with Evan would be another act of infidelity. Evan had made it easy for me to return and I pledged my fidelity to him from that time on.

~

I sobbed as I pulled away from the cliff and I sobbed all the way home. I sobbed on the phone to Evan telling him about Sally. I sobbed when I called our parents. Evan came home from work and held me, letting me wet his shoulder with my tears. I didn't tell him my tears were for Gordon.

joel

Sally had a sweet little voice and wanted to sing. She worried about getting older and losing her looks, so maybe performing was a way for her to get back into the spotlight, her own version of the rose window of Chartres. She liked to tell me that her songs had messages, but if they did that message was pretty garbled. Lots of weak leftover images of butterflies and crystals and all that hippie druggy stuff about karmas and convergences, but she also had these songs about people she'd been in her past lives, a notion that charmed me though I don't believe in past lives and I'm not sure Sally really did either. There was a delphic oracle, a woman burned as a witch in Salem, a young Druid priestess at Stonehenge, that sort of thing. Thank goodness there were no Cleopatras or Marie Antoinettes. The songs were monologues. She'd probably read Robert Browning in one of her college courses.

Sally was smiling this iffy but engaging off-center smile when Evan introduced us, trying to be bold, risky, but with a twitch of self doubt built in. She had to lift her head to talk to me, a small neat head on a long graceful neck. She knew how to tilt her pretty chin. The attempt was coquettish but her stance was more confrontational than coquettish.

"So what did you think?" she asked the day after the introductions.

Stu, the owner of the bar, had invited me to come to her audition. I guess because I'd asked him to give her a chance and if she was really bad he wanted me to know it right away. She wasn't really bad. She was nervous as hell but okay. "Stu liked it," I said. "I have a feeling he's going to ask you to come in and do a set this evening." Stu'd gotten a phone call in the middle of a song and had ducked into his office.

"That's not what I asked."

"Why ask me? I'm not Stu."

"Because I know you exert some influence here. How or why I don't know. If I'm terrible, you're here to find out and Stu won't have to apologize for not hiring me."

"You're long on theory," I said. "Maybe it's not like that at all."

"But it is," she said. Her eyes had hardened, malachite, not so much at me as in an effort to protect herself from hurt.

"I liked it," I said. "Your range isn't large but you deliver a song in a nice personal way. You're in the song. It's appealing."

She shrugged and tried for a noncommittal look. She'd hoped for more. I'd like to have given her more but I was trying for honesty. Anna was ruthlessly honest and after all my years with her some of it had rubbed off.

Stu came back. She sang another song, the one about the woman being burned at the stake, a dirge thing but with a nice melodic line. Her playing wasn't great but it was clean. "Yeah, yeah," said Stu when it was over. "See you tonight. Nine. Don't make me wait."

I walked with her out into the street. Two in the afternoon. I had a client in half an hour. "Can I buy you lunch?" she said.

"I don't want you to think I'm not appreciative."

"Yeah, yeah," I said imitating Stu and she laughed. We ate a sandwich sitting at some tables on the sidewalk. She had a glass of wine to celebrate. I had iced tea. I don't drink much and never when I work.

She tilted her head again. In the sunlight, all those wrinkles appeared and sun blotches showed through the makeup. "I needed this gig," she said. "I need money but I also need some assurance that I'm not nuts, that I can do this."

"Looks like you proved it. Stu doesn't hire everybody who walks in the door."

I could see her wanting to say something like not unless

they're friends of Joel's but thinking the better of it. "I'm going to believe that," she said and held her glass up to the light.

All at once I felt relieved. I didn't realize that I'd had something riding on that audition too. "Believe it," I said and put my hand over hers. I didn't get the coquette look from her but a quick furtive glance trying to read my intentions, a cautiousness that told me she'd had a lot of bad experience with men. At that point I wanted to be the different man for her. There was a rush then. A quickening of my pulse, nothing like the way I'd felt with Anna, that sudden buoyancy that told me I was in love, but a quickening still. With Sally I felt protectively interested, and she did stir me. She had when she brushed back her hair with her long nervous fingers after we'd said our first hello. Her eyes had looked so tired and she'd been trying so hard to impress me with her independence, her self-assurance.

~

She found a funky little cottage to rent. Nothing in it worked. The refrigerator heated food and the stove only had one burner that cooked. We made love there the first time and I had nightmares later that I was being gassed. It was the mildew. "It's cheap," she said. "I need to save my money."

"Listen, I've got a cabin up on the coast. Mostly I stay in my condo in town but when I need some quiet to work I go there. Why don't you settle in the cabin."

She shook her head. "No, I'm not doing things like that any more—moving in after the first fuck."

"Don't say fuck." I put my finger over her lips.

"I'll say what I please."

"It's just such an ugly word. We made love last night."

She sighed. "I don't think so."

"You're trying to hurt me."

She smiled. "It was very nice, but it wasn't love."

"You don't know that."

She got up and went to the window and pulled the curtain. A mottled beam of sunlight fell on her breasts, on the hollow of her stomach, on the thatch of her pudendum. I've always felt that a beam of sunlight confers a blessing—not that I would have used the word *blessing* before Anna. Sally crossed her arms above her head and shifted position. "It's hard letting myself get into something like this again."

"Like this? This is new. There's never been a *like this* before." It wasn't a line. I felt my heart expand. I felt hopeful.

She put her hands behind her head and stretched and the sun rippled over her.

"Come back to bed," I said.

She did.

evan

according to Mattie, Gordon painted enormous canvases with big swathes of color. "Sprawling and intense at the same time," was the way she'd described them, but I never saw any. Gordon had been in art school with Mattie and he moved up to the country near here and made a studio out of an old barn in an apple orchard. He had a wife and three little children and they lived in the farm house while Gordon lived in the barn where he spent his days painting. He was just on the verge of recognition in a big way said Mattie—really big—much bigger than what she called her "minor success" of selling well in a good but not particularly important gallery. According to Mattie, New York had been sniffing around Gordon. He'd had a one-man show in San Francisco which had done well enough for him to move to the country and do nothing but paint. She admitted he was a little fanatic. He'd barricaded the barn as if expecting a siege. Literally. With boards across the doors and padlocks. As if someone might come in and tear his brush out of his hand. He was one of those natural light painters. He'd knocked out part of the roof and installed long windows. When he finished for the day he liked to drive down to the 7-Eleven and buy a six-pack and then cruise the countryside in this old Chevy pickup.

I met him once, and only once, in the 7-Eleven when I'd gone down with Mattie for some ice-cream on a particularly hot night. She hadn't seen him since art school and they appeared pleased to run into each other. He was a short, broad man with thick arms, the kind of guy who chooses wrestling as his sport in high school, with electric chestnut-colored hair and a huge springy beard. I didn't pay much attention because Mattie knows a lot of people in the art scene here. He invited her to see his work and she went, and that's when I learned about how he was living. Again I didn't think much of it. I was working nights then and I guess shortly after that he began coming by.

The first I knew about their affair came one morning when I walked into the kitchen for breakfast. I was working until two then and Mattie always got up early to paint so we didn't see each other until around noon those days. She'd fix a sandwich for herself and bacon and eggs for me. That day she put her sandwich, tuna on whole wheat with the lettuce sticking out—I'll never forget that sandwich because it was what I stared at while she talked—on the table and sat down and without taking a bite said, "I've been having an affair with Gordon for over a year now. He comes for me in the afternoons and we drive around together. Sometimes we drive out to the ocean and talk and sometimes we go to his studio and make love." By that time I was having trouble catching my breath but she just went on talking.

"Lately Gordon's been having these headaches and his vision's been blurring. He went to the doctor and yesterday the doctor told him he has a brain tumor. The doctor gives him a month to live. We've decided to go to Italy together until he dies. He's making arrangements to sell his paintings and provide for his family and with what's left over we'll be able to stay there until it happens. I've told Cammie that I've gotten a fellowship to study at an art institute in Florence and I hope you won't tell her differently. I'm telling you because I love you and you must know the truth."

"You love me?" I was gasping, breathing through my mouth.

She closed her eyes and put her hands in front of her face and nodded.

"And what about him? Do you love him too?"

She nodded again.

"You know I can't stop you," I said. I'd gotten a bit of wind back only now I was sweating.

"I know you won't," she said, taking her hands from her face. I've never seen anyone look so goddammed tragic in my life.

I got up from the table and went into the bathroom and vomited.

~

I was a wild man then, not eating enough, drinking too much, trying to be cheerful for Cammie when all I wanted to do was wail. In less than a month he was dead. I hadn't gotten so much as a postcard from Mattie. I walked in one evening — I was no longer working until after midnight — and found her sitting on the couch staring out of the window. It was July and the dark came late. The trees had years to go before they'd be cut and I remember the way their big black trunks loomed against the fading sky. "I'm just exhausted," she said. "We'll talk later." We never did.

Things changed but not in the way I might have expected. I acquired Mattie's exhaustion as if it were a communicable disease. I had trouble getting out of bed and trouble getting to sleep. I quit one job, took another, and quit that too. Then I got fired from the next, which meant unemployment compensation, not much money but enough to sit around a lot. Mattie began teaching with a vengeance but not painting at all. Cammie, thank God, was busy with junior high school, too busy I hoped to notice how out of sorts we were. Though we rarely talked, Mattie and I continued to make love and not out of habit either but greedily, gorging ourselves at this secret banquet we could still find our way to. Then, after a year, like people recovering from an illness, we began to speak to each other again, but never about Gordon. I wondered then and still do if what happened to us was truly a form of illness. If it was, would we have some immunity from now on or even less resistance in the future?

mattie

i arranged a memorial service for Sally using a minister the funeral home recommended. Our parents, tanned from endless hours of golf in the Arizona sun, flew up and stayed in a motel. "We don't want to impose," my mother said when I argued that I had room at the house.

As soon as they were in the motel room my father pulled a bottle of Scotch from his suitcase, then went for ice. "Your father's not handling this well," my mother said, but I saw no sign of this from either of them. Both appeared composed.

The service itself was a brief event accompanied by some bland but well intentioned words from the minister. The group was composed of Cammie and Evan, my parents, myself, a woman who had been a friend of Sally's in college, and a small dark-haired woman with fine bones and large intelligent eyes, a person I'd never seen before. Joel didn't appear, not that I'd expected him. Neither of my parents cried, though on the way out my mother tripped over the carpet runner in the center aisle and let out an almost animal yelp of pain when her knee hit the floor. No one else cried either, though Cammie sniffled. She'd hardly known Sally but on her visits Sally had always paid attention to Cammie, twining her hair with flowers, teaching her songs, and reading stories whenever Cammie asked. I also didn't cry. The sorrow I felt for Sally took the form of an amnesia in which I didn't actually forget things as much as feared that I would forget them.

~

After my parents flew off, Evan and I rented a charter boat to scatter Sally's ashes in the ocean beyond the headlands. "Be at rest, Sally. I love you," I said, the only words that seemed appropriate. The bits of bone broke the surface and sank while the falling ashes skimmed off on the wind before streaking the water.

"They pulled her out and now we're putting her back," said Evan.

"You don't need to say that," I said.

Evan shrugged and walked to the other side of the boat. As I stood with the empty box the boat lurched, heading back

into the channel. The land ahead looked too green against the
dark gray sky, a violent green.

~

Evan and I had married right after college. We'd been
together most of our senior year, not living together, but
spending time in each other's apartments in the student neigh-
borhood of Berkeley. I studied art and Evan studied history. He
was going to go on to graduate school but never did. I soon
realized that while art was my passion, history had merely
been a course of study for Evan which could just as easily been
any other subject. I'd always been so busy with my painting
that it was difficult for me to make time for anything else. I
loved Evan but was not lost without him. I loved Cammie in
the way I believe mothers love their children, more than anything, but I thought about her as part of myself too, separate
and unique, but me all the same.

Evan had charm, an easy glamorous charm, and wonderful
looks. When I first met him I loved sketching him. He has a
long sinuous athletic body, a shapely head capped with curls,
a narrow straight nose, full lips, and a strong indented chin——a
Greek marble in the flesh. As I found my life in teaching and
painting, Evan found his life in work at one or another un-
demanding job, sports with men friends, bars, maybe an occa-
sional woman. His absences gave me time for my work and I
never begrudged them because I knew always that he loved me
in a solid, undramatic way.

Gordon loved me dramatically, viscerally. Gordon and I could never have been husband and wife because we would have worn each other out. We each wanted to paint, first of all, and when that was done we wanted to fall into a lover's arms to suck back all the juice that painting drew out. Lovemaking was brief and brutal, each pushing the other for more. We seldom spoke. He was not a confidant. He was a physical force that I met with my own physical force. In marriage I think there is always a stronger partner, though the power may shift from time to time. Gordon and I had been equals.

~

That night after the boat trip and the ashes as we lay side by side in bed Evan said, "You've been thinking about him, haven't you, these last days?"

"Yes."

"You were crying for him, not Sally." It was a reproach.

"I didn't cry for him when he died. I couldn't."

"So one of these days you'll get around to crying for Sally?"

"You've a right to be angry. I hurt you. I put a lot at risk. You let me come back."

He sighed. "I needed you. I still do. You don't need me."

"I let Gordon go with those tears," I said. "You have to believe that." I turned to him and put my fingers on his arm and felt his muscle tense under my touch.

"My God, Mattie, I'm trying to," he said rolling onto his side, giving me his back, letting my fingers slide away.

e v a n

the store where I work recently started handling computers because we have to compete with the discount chains, so about a week after Mattie's show they sent me to a workshop on computers in Anaheim. I didn't leave the hotel once during the five days because the hotel was less dismal than the world outside. My room had a view of the Matterhorn, which looked dusty and weary in the morning rather than fresh with alpine optimism.

I have a knack for computers which will probably mean improved job security if I want it but I have no interest in them. When I was young I was good with cards. I won money in college, and at parties I had people oooh and ahhh when I made the right card leap from the deck into my hand. These two abilities may spring from the same source. I no longer do card tricks or try to win at blackjack. When I think back on my life I think of myself as a man with abundant knack but limited enthusiasm. My only long term enthusiasm has been Mattie. I wrote her a postcard from Anaheim, a postcard showing the Matterhorn. "Now that you're a success, maybe your next landscape should be something more challenging— a plaster mountain, perhaps. The triumph of art over artifice." I told myself I was being funny. Mattie likes Disneyland. She and Cammie came here together and rode everything twice.

On my first day back I found Sally waiting for me leaning against the briefcase display. "Your friend Joel is some kind of guy," she said. I had no idea what she meant so I didn't say anything. I just smiled waiting for what would come next.

"No really," she said. "He's got great connections. I came here to invite you and Mattie to the Green Horn tomorrow night. I've got a gig." I looked impressed but felt dubious. Why hadn't she called Mattie to extend this invitation? The Green Horn was a well-known music club about twenty miles south which got acts from San Francisco. "Yeah, I know it's a Tuesday night," she said, "but it's a great place."

"That Joel, some guy," I said.

"You probably think he's bribing people to let me play. He is a powerful figure. Everywhere we go people know him."

"I don't know how the music business works, Sally. I'm glad he's helping."

"I guess Mattie told you that he's got a cabin up on the coast," she said. "I feel very calm and positive there. Joel doesn't go there every night because of work so we both have our time alone but we're getting close, very close. There's a connection. It's a little frightening," she went on. "You probably think he only wants to fuck me but it isn't that at all."

I knew right away that I didn't want to hear any more about this but I didn't have to worry because just when I thought she was about to reveal something more about the two of them she slid into an expression I'd seen before, a disturbing absent expression—eyes in soft focus, jaw slack, lips parted. I put my hand under her chin and lifted it, closing her mouth for her. She looked startled, exactly what I'd hoped for.

"Flies," I said. "They take every opportunity."

She glared. "I can't believe I tried to talk to you."

"What can you expect from a guy who steals bicycles?" I said. "See you tomorrow night."

~

She opened for a locally well-known folksy social protest singer, a hefty woman in her early sixties who belted and was a real crowd pleaser if you got the right crowd. Unfortunately there wasn't much of a crowd yet, right or otherwise. No matter that Sally infuriated me, I didn't want to see her humiliated. I could feel Mattie's tension. "I don't know why she puts herself through this," said Mattie.

I looked around again wondering if I'd missed Joel when we walked in but no. "Maybe she'll be better than we expect."

And she was, though only by inches. She made a great entrance in a long silver dress, her hair pulled back with a rose behind her ear. Her first song was actually perky with some clever lyrics about men and women wanting the same thing but not in the same way. Her voice slid convincingly around the words and she smiled a lot and moved her shoulders. Then she got serious—which in this case meant monotonous. The whispering got old fast. But none of the twenty or so patrons booed or hissed and there was a scattered light applause when she stood up and bowed. Joel still hadn't appeared so I'd expected she'd come out and join us. She didn't.

The crowd arrived for the next act, mostly people in their forties and fifties who'd marched together from one cause to another during the sixties and seventies. They all seemed to know each other and when their singer came out it was old home week. She sang and she was good and warm and funny. Mattie went backstage to find Sally and came back alone. "She's gone. Nobody knows where."

Then Joel arrived looking flustered. He talked to a man at the bar then went backstage and came out alone. If he saw us he didn't acknowledge it. Instead he sat at the bar and had a drink and Mattie and I went home.

The next day Joel came into the store and waited while I

gave a lengthy demonstration on a computer until he could corner me. "Do you have any idea where Sally might be?" he said. He looked as if he hadn't slept much which surprised me because it seemed to indicate that he cared about her welfare. I don't know why but I guess I couldn't imagine anyone actually getting involved with Sally on anything other than a superficial plane.

"She left after her set," I said. "Mattie and I were there for it."

"And I wasn't," he said.

I shrugged.

"I got there late but I don't believe it was that. She knows I get busy. She'd understand that. She wasn't at her cottage or at the cabin. I drove around all night looking for her."

"Maybe you should talk to Mattie. I can give you her office number at the college."

"No. I thought you'd be the one. Sally has some sort of thing about you."

"Me?" Shocked.

"I think Mattie intimidates her. I guess she thinks Mattie intimidates you too."

"I don't know that Sally likes me very much," I said.

It was his turn to shrug. "I just thought you might have some idea."

"She does this," I offered. "She goes away without saying good-bye and disappears for years. It was ten the last time."

"I know. I just thought that maybe things were different now."

"I wouldn't worry."

He sighed and his big shoulders heaved. "I really like her singing you know. Granted her range is narrow but there's a poignancy to her voice. It gets to me."

"Yes," I said. I wanted him to leave. Thank goodness the fellow who'd been looking at the computer had made up his mind and was gesturing to get my attention. "I've got to go."

"Sure, sorry," he said and gave me an eye-to-eye look asking for my cooperation on something, I wasn't sure what, which really upset me. Here was this big physically powerful man showing every sign he wanted to moan or sob or fall to his knees right in front of me. He didn't, thank God. He pulled himself together and hurried out.

~

"Sally was here when I got home," Mattie said. I'd just come in the door. "She'd been drinking—a lot. She said she spent last night in a motel. She thought her performance was so terrible she didn't want to see anyone or talk about it. Instead she wanted to talk about us when we were children."

"It wasn't such a terrible performance," I said.

"I know. I was very positive when I talked to her, but she didn't want to hear. She has this thing about talking about our childhood. You know, she's five years younger than I am so what I remember is very different from what she remembers.

She wanted to talk about school. She was a top student all the way through college. Everything came so easily for her. I had to struggle for every A, for every award. She wanted to talk about a time when she came home with a C in math. In junior high. I told her I had lots of C's. I didn't remember her lonely little C. Then she wanted to talk about boyfriends—about how I always had the boyfriends that all the other girls wanted. She said it was strange because I wasn't the best looking girl by a long shot. I felt under attack. It was all so silly. I made her eat a sandwich and drink some coffee before she left. She said she was on her way to Joel's."

"He'll be relieved," I said and told Mattie about Joel's visit, about his anguish. She listened but didn't appear very interested in Joel.

She poured herself a glass of wine and opened me a beer. "Sally's on a tear again. No telling what's next."

I'd never told Mattie about the way Sally attacked me the night I'd introduced her to Joel or about the bicycle accusation or about fucking her. This wasn't the right time either. "I guess she'll take another trip and it'll be another ten years."

"It was all ridiculous," Mattie said looking out of the window to where the trees, once so huge and oppressive, now seemed destined to be forgotten.

"Even about the boyfriends?" I said it like a tease but naturally something like that made me curious. "I wasn't aware that all the girls wanted me and you won out over them."

"You were extremely handsome," she said. "You also seemed aloof, which made you desirable."

"I was never aloof."

"I learned that later. You just didn't care the way other men did—about things."

"I loved you. I thought I was the one who won out."

"I know," she said. She drank some wine and put the glass down and stared at her hands. She has short blunt fingers with short nails. There's always a trace of paint under the nails or clinging to the cuticles. "Sally must be getting tired," she said.

joel

Sally was at the cabin when I got there on the night after the night of her performance. She apologized for skipping out and I offered my apologies for being late and it felt as if we were back on track. She'd been coming up to the cabin during the middle of the week when I wasn't there but she kept her cottage in town. She cleaned and aired the cabin and took care of things the way she hadn't with her own place. She bought food and re-filled the spice rack. I could tell she wasn't really domestic, but she was making an effort to be and that touched me. I could smell fresh start all over the place. We drank a little wine and listened to Van Morrison and made love, a good evening.

Anna had asked me to move out about three months before I met Sally. I'd been seeing another woman and I'd told Anna, more of that honesty I caught from her, and Anna took it upon herself to meet the woman. "She's completely wrong for you," Anna said. "She's out to destroy herself and she'll take you down with her if you stay with her. You can't help her."

Anna was right, of course, but I kept on seeing the woman. It was a case of lust not love and I knew it and tried to explain it to Anna but she was unmoved. I was still seeing the woman when I met Sally. I didn't tell Anna about Sally at first, but after the scene with Sally over the performance I'd missed I began to think my relationship with Sally might be serious so I decided that I should. I wanted Anna to know how things were.

As soon as I told her about Sally, Anna announced she wanted to meet her, which I guess I'd expected after the last occasion. I called Sally and told her that Anna wanted to get together with her and without me. I'd told Sally a little about Anna but I wasn't sure how she'd take this. "Everything you've told me about her makes me know I'll like her," Sally said. "I've been wanting to meet her, too."

Anna drove up to the cabin. I didn't expect Anna to approve of Sally. It would be safe to say Sally's behavior appeared to me to be much like the previous woman's. It didn't turn out that way.

"I truly liked her," Anna said. I'd asked Anna to lunch after the meeting. She held a piece of French bread from the basket and was slathering butter on it as she spoke. "I think I'd like to bring the boys up and give them a chance to meet her." This took me completely aback.

"But she's a drinker, Anna, and probably self-destructive."

"I understand that but I believe there's hope in Sally's case. Of course, we should never give up hope for anyone, though some people make it difficult. With Sally I believe there's hope. She's capable of loving. I felt that possibility radiating from her. She made me tea and we sat on the couch in front of the wood stove and watched the flames behind the glass. I took her hand and held it while we talked. I think the boys will like her."

The way Anna spoke about the boys meeting Sally made me uneasy. After I'd moved out I continued to visit them and Anna, trying to act as if we were still a normal family, but I could sense their tension each visit and knew they were waiting and watching for what would come next. Eight-year old James had begun having nightmares and Kevin, only six, was picking fights in school. I knew my leaving shattered their sense of an ordered, controllable world, a world I wanted very much to put together again for them and for myself. Even though I was seeing Sally I still believed I'd get back together with Anna. I hadn't managed to work out how this would happen but Anna's talking about Sally meeting the boys sounded a chilly note. I could see Anna pulling away and offering Sally in her place.

At the same time I had a tough murder case on my hands. A wealthy local banker was about to go on trial for murdering his mistress. He'd suspected her of seeing another man. One night he'd parked in a rented car outside her house. When the woman arrived with a man, he waited until they went inside then opened her front door with his key and shot them both— the man, who'd been sitting facing the woman across the coffee table, in the back of the head, the woman in the chest, the head, and then some. He'd emptied the gun on her. The district attorney asked for the death penalty. My defense, with a platoon of psychiatrists testifying to my client's diminished capacity, was to be temporary insanity.

You have to believe in your client to do your work well. This meant I had to believe in crimes of passion. It wasn't hard. Anna's bringing up the idea of Sally meeting the boys sent me into a spin of depression and anxiety. I didn't want to lose Anna. I cared for Sally, even loved her, but I couldn't give up Anna and my sons. I felt my own capacity to make rational judgements diminish. I found myself thinking of ways to spirit Anna and the boys away with me to some remote spot, an island with no way off after the boat that brought us sailed away, a snowed-in cabin in the high Sierras, someplace where I could gather us together until I could convince Anna that staying together was the only possible way for us. I'd ruthlessly use the boys and their desire for stability to force Anna to agree to return to me.

The day after my lunch with Anna I met with my client. I'd asked him before but now I asked him again what it felt like in the minutes before he opened her door and began firing.

"I wasn't there," he said. He was a heavy, balding man of sixty with beefy jowls and washed out gin-colored eyes. He sat with his arms folded on the table across from me, resigned, almost complacent. "I wasn't in my body. I was outside of it all watching myself do these terrible things as if I was seeing myself on television, on one of those little screens in an old console set. Black and white. What my body did was going on without me. I couldn't make myself stop, you understand. I'd been on tranquilizers for weeks before that and one morning I told myself that I needed to stop taking the damn pills. I needed to know how I really felt. When I stopped taking the pills I couldn't stand what I felt. That's all."

"Jesus, that's just awful," I said. I'd heard all this before from him but now the horror of his situation made my head swim. He looked at me, lifted an eyebrow for a moment to see if I'd meant it, and then he looked down when he saw that I did. I'd been thinking about calling a shrink and getting tranquilizers myself but I decided not to. I needed to watch myself, not medicate myself. I didn't see violence in my future but I did see loss, a loss I wasn't prepared to bear, and I knew I'd have brought it on myself. I thought about trying to pray to Anna's God but it seemed shoddy to try to use Him, or Her, against Anna unless I could lay out a convincing argument that Anna's letting me come back was the best thing for Anna. I was a lawyer. I knew how to argue and I knew how to cut a deal but praying was probably not in the picture.

mattie

a couple of days after scattering Sally's ashes I stopped by the gallery to bring in some small un-matted paintings for a client. In one corner of the gallery, studying a landscape, one of a river with vineyards in which the patterns of the land becomes a section of crazy quilt, stood the woman from the service for Sally. When she saw me she smiled, a rather wistful smile, and made her way over.

"I admire your paintings," she said. "Joel bought one of your pieces for his office and I decided I wanted one too."

"That's quite a compliment," I said.

"I'm Anna, Joel's wife." She put out a hand for a very firm shake. Her eyes, violet-blue, were startlingly luminous and sad.

"I've only met Joel once so I couldn't really say I know him."

"Yes, he told me you drove up to tell him about Sally. It was very thoughtful considering how hard the news must have been for you. Joel, as you can imagine, is devastated. He asked me to go to the service in his place. Of course, I would have gone anyway. I was quite fond of Sally. We had some remarkable talks."

"I didn't know," I said. "Sally was very circumspect about Joel."

"She wasn't sure that you'd approve of their relationship. She wanted your approval very much. She talked of you a great deal, what a fine artist you were, how Evan adored you, and lots about Cammie—how sweet and smart she was. Sally held you in awe. And she envied you. She felt she'd botched her life through indecision and poor judgement."

"Can we go somewhere and talk?" I said. I wasn't sure I wanted to hear any of this and I wanted a table between us if I had to. "There's a coffee shop across the street."

"Fine. I'll meet you there, but first I want to buy that painting."

It wasn't inexpensive. I went to the desk and spoke to the young woman and introduced her to Anna. Then I went across the street and ordered a cup of coffee. I really wanted something stronger.

Through the window of the coffee shop I saw Anna come out with the wrapped painting and put it into the trunk of her car. She was a beautiful woman with fine sharp bones and her clothes, a soft gray jacket over black trousers with a silvery blue blouse, were simple and well cut. She sat and ordered tea.

"Joel and I live separately but we're still married," she said as if I'd asked. "He's been married twice before and he doesn't want to let this marriage go but we've both admitted we're not really doing very well together. We have two young children, boys, and he adores them." She smiled that same wistful smile and looked out the window. I was growing less comfortable by the second. "I'd wanted to give him custody of the boys but he didn't seem to think he could do it himself so it's necessary for me to be near." Having said that she leaned forward as if she expected a response.

"You're telling me that you wanted to leave your husband and give up your children?" I leaned back in my chair and she pulled back too.

"I didn't want to leave them completely. I'd have them on the weekends and vacations and so on, but the truth is I don't think I'm really suited to be a mother. Sally met the boys. We had a wonderful picnic at the beach. She seemed to like them immediately and they liked her. Sally couldn't have children herself, you know?"

"I didn't know that." I was surprised she'd never mentioned it.

"One of her lovers gave her gonorrhea which scarred her fallopian tubes."

I had a feeling I knew where this was going. "You know a lot about her and it all rings true. When Sally lived here before, she had a string of men and her judgement wasn't the best. One of them stole her jewelry. She loaned money to another and he made off with it. Another beat her so badly she was hospitalized. She got pregnant with another and wanted to keep the child but he convinced her to have an abortion."

"Yes. Joel's impulse with women is to befriend them. He wants to be the man who's different. He truly wants to be good for them. It rarely works out that way, however."

"I don't know what he and Sally were involved in," I said. "But if it was so benign why was she drinking and driving along the coast that night?"

She raised her hands palms up, an odd gesture that shifted my question out into the ether.

She sighed. "I've seen his goodness."

"And Sally?"

She shook her head. "I believe he loved her. If he'd wanted to marry I'd have been very happy. I should never have married him, never had children."

"And Sally could have bailed you out?"

She winced then smiled, the wistful smile yet again. "In a manner of speaking. I believed she was willing."

"And Joel?"

"He did love her."

I looked away into the glare on the street. The white walls

of the gallery burned with light. A block of blue shadow from the awning cut away the light at a sharp angle.

"Then why did she plunge over the cliff into the ocean?"

"You're wrong to think of it as suicide. She'd been drinking, true, but the road is hazardous."

"Has Joel told you what went on, why early one morning my sister should take it upon herself to drive over a cliff?"

"He was at the cabin alone waiting for her but she didn't come. About two she drove into the driveway but when he went out she backed up and drove away."

Maybe this was true. I wasn't sure what knowing it meant.

"Sally was troubled and questioning," Anna said, sitting back in the chair and folding her hands on the table. I sensed a shift at that moment as if she'd pulled away and was somewhere on the edge of a field looking at Sally from over a fence.

I turned my gaze outside again to the diagonal of shade under the awning of the gallery. I closed my eyes.

"I can see I've tired you," I heard her say. "I've burdened you and I'm sorry. I can see now that it was my own need to tell you this, to speak to you, more than my belief that you needed to know that made me come. But I do love the painting. I'm happy I have it." I heard her chair scrape and I opened my eyes. She was standing. She held out her hand and I took it. Her hand was cool.

On my way from the gallery I drove by Joel's office, a renovated Victorian with a signboard outside listing a string of lawyers. When I'd arrived at his cabin door the day of Sally's death he'd looked as if he'd been waiting for just such news. If I was thinking about walking into his office now and asking what had really gone on between him and Sally, I gave it up. The same weariness I'd felt on the plane back from Rome overtook me and it was all I could do to get home.

Inside my bedroom I drew the draperies and, still dressed, crawled under the covers and slept. I knelt on something hard, with my hand reaching down into the water, a neighbor's swimming pool where Sally and I had played when we were young. I could tell even in the semi-darkness, that the pool was dank and scummy with the scent of rot hovering over it. At the bottom lay Sally, eerily white, face up, holding her breath. I lowered my hand and touched her hair but when I grabbed the hair, and pulled it to get Sally to the surface the hair came away in my hands. I sat on the edge of the pool staring at a handful of glossy seaweed, which became eels, which became black satin ribbons.

joel

Sally was sitting on a rug in front of the fire strumming her guitar and whispering along with the chords when I pushed open the cabin door. I remember the words because she sang the refrain over and over as if wanting to get it right. *The mist rises softly from the cold sea / The horizon appears on the edge of the world / Here comes my boat, I sing to the sky / Please take me to him, I sing to the sea.*

"Very nice," I said sitting on the sofa beside her, "very nice."

She lifted her face for my kiss. She looked amazingly contented, serene really. I'd never seen her this way.

"You look especially lovely," I said. I kissed her forehead, her lips. I knelt beside her and kissed her throat. The firelight cast a rose hue on her profile, highlighting her hair. Her long fingers toyed with the strings.

"Anna is so wonderful," she said. "I feel as if I've known her all my life. I hadn't expected so much affection from her. She brought the boys up here for a picnic this afternoon and we had such a good time. They're great kids. I mean, you are so lucky."

My heart stopped. Sally turned my head and touched my lips with hers. She took my hand and placed it over her breast.

"Feel my heart," she said. "It's a glad heart. Anna isn't going to stand between us."

I'd begun to sweat. I pulled back. "You've quite a fire in that stove," I said, taking off my jacket. Her blouse fell open and I caught a glimpse of her small pale breast, the bud-like nipple. She smiled and touched my cheek and got up and went to the kitchen and came back with a bottle of red wine and poured us each a glass. I took the cool glass stem and swirled the wine, then sipped. I took another sip.

"Nice wine isn't it? I thought we'd need something special tonight to celebrate."

"Very nice." I couldn't taste a thing. It could have been Kool-Aid. I took another sip and put the glass on the hearth. She reached out her hand and pulled me down on the rug beside her and put her head against my shoulder. I could feel contentment coursing through her like a muted purr and I felt absolutely awful. Sally began singing again and I saw Anna standing on the bow of a boat, the only one on the boat, smiling to herself, inward, self-contained. A wind filled the sail and sent the boat skimming over the choppy waves. On the distant horizon the sun lay half submerged, either rising or setting.

After a while Sally's hand began stroking my neck, my shoulders, unbuttoning my shirt. She guided my hand to her breast. I kissed her cheek, her ear, her hair. Her smell was a musk laced with sandalwood and warm flesh. I picked up my wine glass, dipped my finger, and painted her nipples with wine, then sucked them until she moaned. She lay on the floor and pulled me on top of her and I went into her over and over, deeper and deeper.

We managed to get to bed and I fell immediately into a heavy dense forest of dreams where animals changed shapes and wouldn't reveal themselves to me no matter how long I pursued them. I woke when the door from the bedroom to the living room, still lit by firelight, closed. I reached out and felt the space beside me empty but still warm. I dropped back to sleep.

I woke again and heard her moving in the living room. I got up and found her sitting in front of the dying fire with a glass of orange juice except I knew it wasn't just orange juice. She kept a bottle of vodka and a carton of juice in the refrigerator but she'd never drunk anything but wine or beer with me and always moderately. I'd decided to believe her drinking wasn't serious. Her face was streaked with tears which had managed somehow to create rivulets down her cheeks, smearing her mascara and giving her the look of a forlorn clown.

"What's going on?" I sat beside her. She shook her head and turned from me. I put my hand under her chin and tried to turn her back to face me. She wrenched her head away and flung out her hand hitting me in the chest. I sat back. "Sally," I said softly. "Sally, it's me, Joel."

"We don't have a future, Joel. You got this anxious look when I told you that Anna had brought the boys up. That really bothered you. You don't want me in her place. I tried to believe it was something else but I knew it wasn't."

"Listen, Sally, Anna's already left me. I don't think she'll have me back no matter what."

"But she could have you back? It's still possible?"

"I love you, Sally." I'd told her that before and I meant it. A man can love two women though he may love one more. I hoped it would be enough.

"But you want her to take you back?"

I nodded my head, that dangerous honesty again.

She sighed and closed her eyes. When she let out her breath her shoulders slumped and her head fell forward.

"We could have a future," I said, telling myself I wasn't sure it wasn't true. Perhaps we could. My God, I didn't want to hurt her.

"I don't know," she murmured.

"I love you," I said again and took the drink out of her hand

and led her to bed where I folded her against me the way a child would fold a doll. She didn't resist but didn't help, either. I held her hand. It lay limp and cold inside mine.

The next morning we had toast and coffee, our usual breakfast together, and I left. She looked wan but made an effort to be cheerful. After work that evening, instead of going to the condo as I usually did, I drove up to the cabin. I didn't know what I hoped for. I wasn't allowing myself to think things through. When I'd told Sally I loved her, though I did, I'd felt a wave of despair surge inside my chest. A commitment to Sally would mean giving up hope for a reunion with Anna, a reunion which, considering how obdurate Anna could be, was probably not going to happen anyway.

Anna has told me that I have a terrible fear of being alone. I always need a woman and I never am ready to give up one until I have another securely in place. On the evidence I'd have to agree that this is true. I certainly didn't want to be without Anna but if I couldn't have Anna I didn't want to lose Sally as well.

When I got to the cabin I found that Sally had straightened up and vacuumed and even filled several Mason jars with huge bouquets of wild-flowers—lupine, paintbrush, iris, delphinium. Flowers on the coffee table, on the stereo, on the kitchen table, on the dresser in the bedroom. I thought of her in the field below the house gathering these, her head bent, bright in the sunlight, and I took in a long, relieved breath.

Perhaps everything was all right after all. I called her cottage to thank her but there was no answer. I didn't worry. She liked to go out, take walks. She liked to drive up and down the coast. I knew there were a couple of bars she stopped in to have a drink and play the jukebox. "I go to the places that have Patsy Cline on the jukebox," she'd told me once. "I check out the jukebox first and if there's no Patsy Cline, I never go back."

She didn't appear when it got dark but that wasn't unusual either. She may have thought I'd stay in town. Our arrangements for meeting at the cabin were purposefully loose. I drafted a memorandum for my accused murderer and managed not to insert myself inside his cluttered miserable mind. I called again and she was there. She'd gone for a drive. "I'm just checking in," I said. "And I want to thank you for the flowers."

"You probably think it looks like a funeral parlor," she said.

"Not mine, I hope." I tried to laugh but there was an edge to her voice. She'd been drinking again.

"It was just a whim."

"And a good one. They bring into the house all the freshness and promise of spring."

She paused. I could hear her breathing. "That's very nice," she said finally. "That's a nice thing to say."

"I mean it."

"Then double thank you."

"What are you going to do?" I asked. I didn't want her to hang up feeling hurt. I heard her yawn.

"It's nearly eleven o'clock," she said. "I usually go to bed about now." She sounded truly tired, not hurt or edgy now, just tired.

"Sweet dreams," I said.

"Sweet dreams," she echoed.

About two o'clock I heard a car drive up and I knew it would be Sally. There was a fisherman's bar down the coast where she liked to drink, a noisy friendly place. It closed at two. I got on my robe and opened the front door and turned on the porch light. I saw her sitting in the car making no move to get out. The light lit only the lower half of her face. "Sally," I called, "Are you all right? Come on in?" I began to walk toward the car. When I did, I saw her throw it into gear and tear out of the driveway in reverse. On the road she headed north, not south in the direction of her cottage.

I didn't sleep. I waited an hour and called the cottage but she didn't answer. I thought about driving down there, but somehow I couldn't bring myself to do it. I'd seen a set of her chin, an anger, a determination. She would know it was me calling and not answer, I told myself. When Mattie appeared that morning to tell me what had happened I realized that I couldn't have done anything anyway unless I'd managed to stop her driving out of the driveway.

After Mattie pulled away I finished the vodka in the refrigerator. There hadn't been much. Then I drank a couple of beers and paced. I hadn't gone in to work that day and I hadn't

known why at the time. Now I knew that I'd been waiting—
for Sally to come back or for Mattie to arrive. The liquor did
nothing except give me a headache, which in a way I appreci-
ated because everything else felt numb. In the middle of the
afternoon I gathered all the flowers she'd picked and drove
down the coast. The spot was easy to find. It was the spot anyone serious about looking for a place to go over a cliff into the
ocean would pick. A wide outside curve to gather speed and a
sheer drop on the other side. There were some orange police
cones on the shoulder, and tire tracks showed on the low dirt
berm. I looked down and swayed with vertigo. The car was
still down there. The tide was in and waves lapped up as far as
the tires. I took the flowers out of the car and let them drop
one by one. The flowers fell like bright confetti until a gust of
wind blew them against the wall of the cliff, after which they
drifted in the air slowly south, missing the car completely.

anna

the boat with Joel and the boys floated either in the air or on the water. From the porch of the cabin where I sat watching it was hard to tell. The steam from my cup of coffee rose as white as the mist on the lake. We were four spirits, insubstantial and hushed in the wavery morning light. This was not the cabin by the coast but one Joel had rented in the Sierras. We were here for a month practicing how to be a family again. Even the children were awkward. We bumped into each other when we moved around and forget our lines. We smiled and backed away, mumbled apologies, and gestured to show that we'd get it right eventually.

~

Joel had come to me late on the day of the accident. He'd been drinking but the liquor had no calming effect on him. If anything it had made him more agitated. I led him into the study and tried to get him to sit but he paced instead.

"We can't just assume it's suicide," I said.

"We can't just assume it but it is a possibility. No, more than that, a probability. It all got out of hand."

"It could have been an accident. It's a terrible road. She'd been drinking. She drove it at other times when she'd been drinking. She told me that. She was going too fast and misjudged the curve."

"You want to think that. Then you don't have to accept part of the blame," he said turning and going to the window that looked over the back yard. There was nothing to see but a swing set and a few patio chairs but he seemed intent on studying it.

I'd expected him to look for blame and I'd expected him to take it on for both of us. "I'm responsible for her disappointment," I said. "I accept that. I encouraged her. I offered the boys."

"Yes," he said, wheeling on his heel to glare at me. "Yes, you did, my lovely little innocent. You certainly did get involved, didn't you."

"I had no idea it wouldn't turn out well."

"Of course you didn't. You couldn't. You never consulted anyone. You just assumed that because you wanted it to be that way, you could make it happen. One of your saints probably gave you the go ahead."

"That's not fair."

"What's fair? Sally's dead. A fragile spirit is dead." He began to sob, huge choking sobs that set his chest heaving.

"You must know how sorry I am," I said, trying to take his arm, to make him sit. "How terribly, terribly sorry."

He raised his fist and hammered the desk. "Dammit, dammit, dammit. Of course, you're sorry but it doesn't do any good to be sorry now. It's just too damn late." Then he dropped to his knees and put his head on the seat of the chair and began to moan. I tiptoed over and knelt beside him and stroked his head. He continued to moan. I heard the gate to the yard swing open and through the window I saw the boys lugging their backpacks and heading to the back door on the way in from soccer practice. I closed the study door on Joel and went to meet them.

"Kevin made a goal," James said looking up at me, his face burnished by fraternal pride. Kevin shrugged and grinned.

I bent and kissed the top of Kevin's head, "Congratulations, champ." He shrugged again. James was a natural athlete while Kevin, who tended to daydream, usually stumbled through a game noticing birds and clouds, almost anything but the action going on around him. Then I gave James a hug. "Daddy's in the study," I said, "and he can't be disturbed."

When they'd gone to their rooms to clean up I sat at the table trying not to cry tears I couldn't imagine how to explain to them. How could I not want to be a mother? How could I want to let them go? I didn't understand it myself. The boys were numinous creations, small vessels of grace and love, sacred gifts given to me. How could I turn my back on them? I heard the sound of a Nintendo game in the bedroom but instead of calling up to turn it off and get ready for dinner I stayed where I was, in the gathering darkness, with my hands open palms up on the table. "Help me," I whispered. "Help me, help me, help me."

A week later I received a letter from Mark. I hadn't heard from him since I'd said good-bye on the night of the dance but I'd known he could always reach me because we retained certain friends and connections from that time. Mark wrote to tell me that he'd married and that his first child had just been born. He'd been in the delivery room. He wept. He said he'd heard I too was married and he hoped that I was happy. He'd never stopped thinking of me, he said, but he didn't mention the word regret, so perhaps that emotion had nothing to do with his remembrances.

I'd already made a decision to return to life with Joel when the letter appeared. Mark's message had nothing to do with that decision although in its way I saw the letter as Mark's belated blessing of my marriage.

~

Keeping my eyes on the figures in the boat, not wanting to let them fade from my sight, I drank my coffee. A silver flick of fishing line whipped through the air and I thought I heard the tiny plunk as it landed. Yesterday the boys each caught a trout. When I came to the end of the dock to greet them, they held the fish up for my approval with a shared air of grave accomplishment. Joel had sought my eyes over their heads. He wanted my approval too, and I gave it. I held his eyes with mine for a moment more. I wanted his forgiveness, and he gave it. For dinner last night, Joel and the boys fried the trout which we all ate with the proper reverence and compliments.

evan

Cammie had a few days between the end of the school year and the departure of her flight to Florence to attend a summer language institute so she spent the time with us. In the evenings she and Mattie kept their heads together on the sofa in the living room, going through books and making lists. The lists concerned what she would need to bring but mostly what sights she should she see once she got there. These she expected Mattie to supply since Mattie had, after all, been to Italy, and surely had some sort of expertise. Last night as they talked I thought I could hear the strain in Mattie's voice as she tried to fabricate Italy for Cammie's benefit, and I found myself listening because I've never known what she'd actually done there.

While Cammie took notes, Mattie talked about the Botti-
cellis in the Uffizi, Verrocchio's David in the Podesta Palace,
about Ghiberti's doors to a baptistry somewhere—stuff that
sounded like standard guidebook fare, facts you might hear on
public television. As I listened, I noticed a sudden change in
her voice mid-sentence. She stopped mid-way across the
Piazza della Signoria and her voice took on a gentle hesitation
in which I heard an overwhelming sadness, a sadness which I
hoped Cammie would hear as a simple nostalgia. "If I were
you, I'd walk a lot," Mattie said. "I'd walk and walk and make
sure to steal some flowers from a nobleman's garden."

It was such a change of tone that Cammie looked at her
startled, then laughed. "I like that, Mom," she said.

"I thought you would," said Mattie.

The next morning while Mattie painted, Cammie and I
rode our bikes up and down the nearby hills and then down
into town for coffee and muffins. Cammie's in much better
shape than I am but I kept up with her and we were both good
and sweaty when we took a table on the deck of the local coffee shop. I still call it a coffee shop, which it used to be, only
now it has those gleaming hissing machines and serves espresso
and cappuccino and such things and very good pastries.

"You don't want to drink too many of these and then get
tired of them by the time you hit Italy," I said as she ordered
her caffè latte. She gave me a look of scorn, as if such a thing
were impossible.

"I'm going to be hopelessly sophisticated when I get back. I'll say ciao to everyone and wave backward." She tossed her hair. It hung to her shoulders and it swished and jiggled at the same time. A lot of young men would be watching that hair, I thought with no small amount of trepidation. Which made me think of my own days of hair watching, particularly Mattie's hair, hair that hung all the way to the middle of her back and rippled like a glistening brown river when she swung it from side to side.

She's cut it since because it's easier to keep neat she says— something I've never understood. I can't forget how it was then. I'd loved Mattie's hair so much that I learned to braid it. It was a summer evening and she was visiting my house which for some reason was completely empty of all roommates. We sat on the back porch, Mattie in front of me with her back to me, my legs out on either side of her. We'd just made love— maybe our tenth time in all since we'd met and we were still recovering from the awe of it as the sun made its way into the neighbor's plum tree. Turning to me she'd demonstrated how to make a braid by pulling her hair over her shoulder and weaving it in and out. Then it was my turn. That she would allow me to do something as intimate as braid her hair struck me as an incredible privilege, and with each weave of one of the three spills of hair into the other two I felt I was a man performing a sacred ritual. I remember mouthing her name, *Mattie, Mattie, Mattie* as I wove, making her name my chant, my prayer. I knew what I was doing, as sure of it as anything I'd ever done. I was braiding myself into Mattie and Mattie into me for ever and ever, and the best part was I knew the charm of the braid would work.

a
minus
tide

mattie

"i slept with Sally once," Evan said. We lay in bed looking at the moon, a huge looming globe drifting like a wish in a sky the trees had once obscured.

I heard the pain in his voice, the risk he felt he was taking with this confession, but I couldn't summon a bit of emotion about it. I couldn't remember if I'd suspected it once or if she'd told me. I seemed to have known it for a long time and kept that knowledge in a place I couldn't reach. "She cared for you," I said. "She always told me that I'd gotten the best there was because you truly loved me."

"I don't know that she felt that way," he said. "It might have been true once but at the time we slept together she was pretty upset with me. To me it was all over this misunder-standing that had come between us. She never saw it the way I did. In fact, she brought the whole incident up right after she got here this last time. She believed that I'd stolen this bicycle she had when the truth was she'd told me to take the damn thing and trade it for some dope, which I did."

"Forget it, Evan. It was years ago. Why bring it up now?"

"Because I betrayed you then and I betrayed her too. I'm only just understanding that."

"We all wind up betraying the people we love at some time," I said, moving to get closer to him, to feel his skin against mine. "If we're lucky they forgive us."

"She got hysterical and started screaming about this bike she said I'd stolen. She looked absolutely mad, her eyes roll-ing around. I pushed her and she sat down and we smoked the dope and then we wound up together. It was just sex though—enjoyable but hollow. I couldn't feel anything for her, you see. Then's when I failed her. That's what I feel bad about, not about the bike business."

"Let it go. Please."

"It still doesn't make any sense but I needed to tell you. I needed you to know."

He sounded so anguished. I knew he wanted to talk about it even though I didn't want to hear. "Where did you make love to Sally?" I thought that if I could picture it I could begin to see it through his eyes and maybe see what he wanted me to understand.

"In that trailer."

"In that dreadful trailer?" I said as the memory of the trailer with the India print spreads over the window, the smell of marijuana and spilt wine and incense—all of it already old then, the detritus of an unhappy attempt at fantasy—appeared in my mind like a photograph from the very distant past complete with water stains and yellowed curled edges. It was so awful I wanted to laugh.

"It's so hard to let things go," he said, almost a groan.

"I couldn't save her," I said, putting my head on his chest so that he could wrap his arms around me. I felt my tears for Sally begin in that spot right behind my breast bone. He tightened his hold on me and I placed my hands over his.

Beyond the window where the trees had stood I saw a vast emptiness. I would never have predicted how once so much could be there and now not be there at all.